WALT DISNEY'S

THE JUNGLE BOOK

ADAPTED BY ANNIE AUERBACH

This is the story of the young Man-cub Mowgli and his adventures in the jungle. Read along with me as we embark on an exciting adventure. You will know it is time to turn the page when you hear this sound.... Just follow along, and enjoy this wonderful tale about Mowgli and friends!

One day, a panther named Bagheera discovered a half-sunken boat deep in the jungle. Inside the boat was a baby boy!

"It's a Man-cub," Bagheera realized. He knew the nearest Man-village was far away, so he brought the Man-cub to a family of wolves.

It didn't take long for the wolves to take him in and raise him as one of their own.

The boy became known as Mowgli, and for ten years, he lived happily in the jungle. Then one day, news spread that the fierce tiger, Shere Khan, had returned to the jungle. He hated Man and would surely kill Mowgli.

The wolf pack elders met and decided that Mowgli must leave, for his own safety, as well as for the pack's.

"I know a Man-village where he'll be safe," said Bagheera.

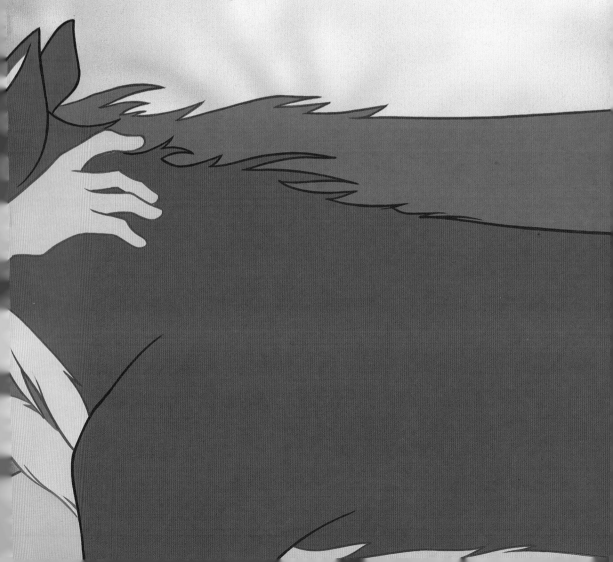

Mowgli resisted, but in the end, he went with
Bagheera. Towards evening, the two climbed a tree to
settle down for the night. Just as Bagheera was drifting
off to sleep, Kaa the snake appeared!

"Sssay now, what have we here?" said Kaa.
"A delicious Man-cub!"

Kaa hypnotized Mowgli as he coiled his tail
around the Man-cub's body. Luckily, Bagheera awoke
and hit Kaa on the head, making the snake release
Mowgli. Kaa slithered away, with a knot in his tail
and a very bad headache!

The next morning, Mowgli still refused to go to the Man-village. "Oh, that does it," Bagheera said, frustrated. "From now on, you're on your own!"

Mowgli wandered into the jungle alone. Soon he met Baloo, a fun-loving, cheerful bear. Baloo and Mowgli became fast friends.

"You're gonna make one swell bear!" said Baloo, proudly, as they floated down the river together.

Suddenly, Mowgli was snatched up into the trees by some mangy monkeys. Baloo did his best to get Mowgli back, but nothing worked. Finally, Baloo shouted to Bagheera for help.

The monkeys took Mowgli to the ancient ruins to meet King Louie. The king wanted to know the secret of man's red fire.

"But I don't know how to make fire," Mowgli replied.

Bagheera and Baloo were hiding nearby.

"Fire? So that's what that scoundrel is after!" said Bagheera.

Quickly, a plan to save Mowgli was hatched and underway. Baloo dressed up as a female monkey, but soon his disguise fell apart—right in front of King Louie! It was a push-and-pull fight for Mowgli. The ancient ruins started to fall apart as Mowgli, Bagheera, and Baloo barely escaped.

That night, while the Man-cub slept, Bagheera convinced Baloo that Mowgli was not safe in the jungle.

Baloo agreed, but was sad to have to send him away. "I love that kid," he said. "I love him like he was my own cub."

"Then think what's best for Mowgli, and not yourself," Bagheera said gently.

When Mowgli found out about the plan the next morning, he ran off.

Bagheera and Baloo had to find Mowgli before Shere Khan did. There was one creature who knew exactly where the Man-cub was—Kaa! Up in a tree, the snake was doing his best to trap Mowgli again.

Suddenly Shere Khan
appeared below.
"I'm searching for a Man-cub," he said,
trying to threaten Kaa.
As Kaa was forced to show his coils to
Shere Khan, Mowgli escaped.

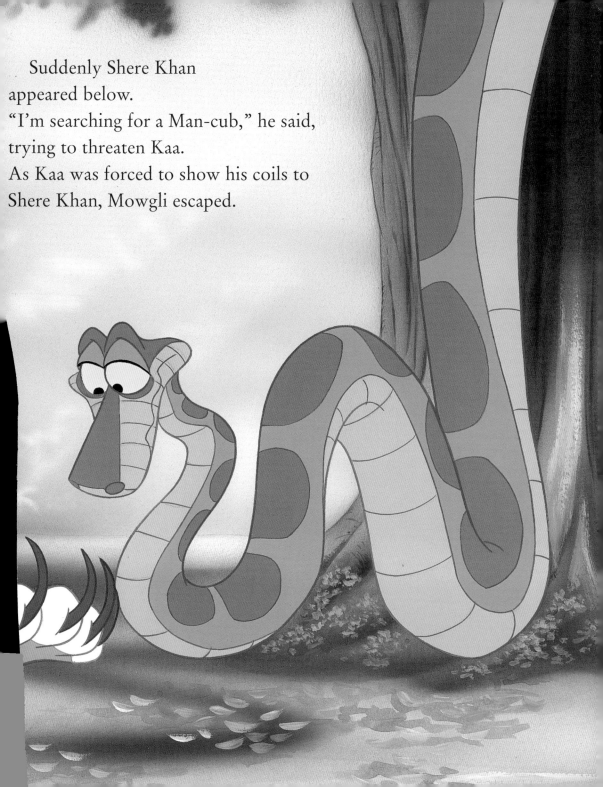

In a clearing, Mowgli met up with some vultures, and then came face to face with Shere Khan.

"You don't scare me," Mowgli said firmly. "I won't run from anyone."

Shere Khan was about to pounce on the Man-cub, but Baloo had grabbed the tiger's tail! The vultures swooped in and picked up Mowgli.

"Let go!" cried Mowgli. "Baloo needs help!"

CRACK! Lightning struck a nearby tree. The tree burst into flames.

Then Buzzie the vulture revealed a secret to Mowgli: "Fire. That's the only thing old Stripes is afraid of."

With all his courage, Mowgli grabbed a burning branch and attached it to Shere Khan's tail.

"Yeow!!!" the terrified tiger screamed and ran into the jungle.

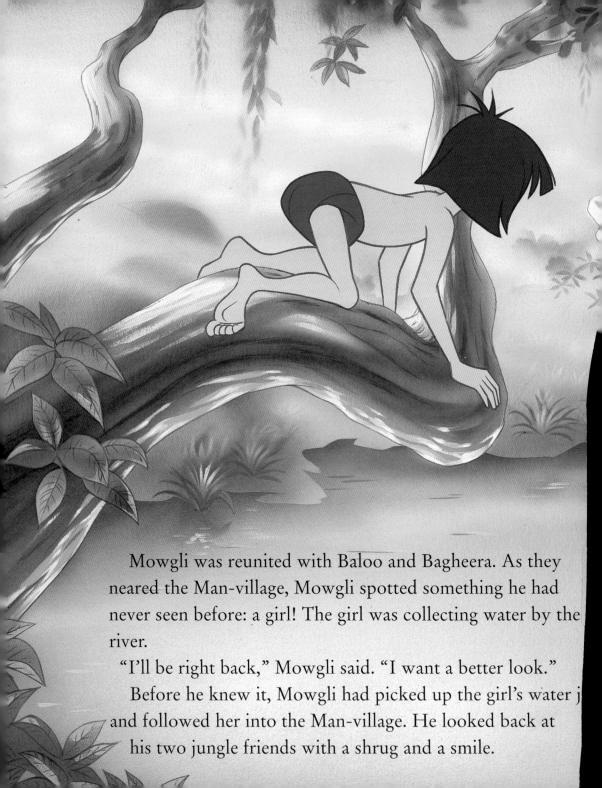

Mowgli was reunited with Baloo and Bagheera. As they
neared the Man-village, Mowgli spotted something he had
never seen before: a girl! The girl was collecting water by the
river.

"I'll be right back," Mowgli said. "I want a better look."

Before he knew it, Mowgli had picked up the girl's water j
and followed her into the Man-village. He looked back at
his two jungle friends with a shrug and a smile.

Bagheera tried to comfort Baloo.

"Mowgli is where he belongs now."

"Yeah, I guess you're right. But I still think he'd make one swell bear," said Baloo. Then he grabbed Bagheera around the waist and they danced into the jungle.

"Come on, Baggy, buddy. Let's get back to where we belong!"